ONCE MORE...

The Gaskitts!

First published 2003 by Walker Books Ltd
87 Vauxhall Walk, London SE11 5HJ

This edition published 2018

2 4 6 8 10 9 7 5 3 1

Text © 2003 Allan Ahlberg
Illustrations © 2003 Katharine McEwen

The right of Allan Ahlberg and Katharine McEwen to be identified
as author and illustrator respectively of this work has been asserted by
them in accordance with the Copyright, Designs and Patents Act 1988

This book has been typeset in Stempel Schneidler,
Cafeteria, Tapioca and Kosmik

Printed in China

British Library Cataloguing in Publication Data:
a catalogue record for this book
is available from the British Library

ISBN 978-1-4063-8166-5

www.walker.co.uk

Allan Ahlberg

The Cat Who got Carried away

illustrated by
KATHARINE MᶜEWEN

WALKER
BOOKS

USEFUL MAPS

Contents

In This Grand and Gripping

Puff!

Gasp!

Mr Gaskitt

spends most of

his time hoovering.

There's a good
reason, though.

Gus and Gloria

have a lot of running to do.

Gaskitts Story

Mrs Gaskitt

hardly ever gets

out of bed.

Why is that?

And Horace -

poor Horace! - ends up ...

in a pet shop!

£5?
I'm a bargain!

£5

★★★ Also Starring ★★★

A rat named **Randolph,**

a guinea pig named **Maurice**

and a teacher named **Mrs Fritter**

(who sometimes falls over).

Not to mention a mysterious

gang of... But more of them later.

ON WITH THE STORY!

Chapter One
The Barking Pram

Early one evening the Gaskitts were at home

sitting side by side on Mr and Mrs Gaskitt's bed.

All except Mrs Gaskitt – she was in bed.

Why is that?

It's only half past seven.

Anyway, there they were

drinking tea,

eating biscuits

and looking at the

family photo album.

There was a photo of Gus and Gloria as babies,

a photo of Horace as a kitten and a photo of

Mr and Mrs Gaskitt ... dancing.

"On our honeymoon," said Mr Gaskitt.

"But what about us?"

"Were we born then?"

the children cried.

"Not quite," said Mrs Gaskitt.

"We had the house to ourselves."

"Yes." Mr Gaskitt smiled.

"It was delightful."

(Gloria punched him.)

"I mean boring."

Boring!
Boring!
Boring!

(And Gus hit him

with a pillow.)

Meanwhile, Horace was outside

sitting on the garden wall

watching the world go by.

He saw a boy on a bike,

a boy on a skateboard,

a woman in a car

and, finally,

on the other side of the road,

a man absolutely *whizzing* along

with a really old pram.

And the strange thing was,

which Horace noticed,

the strange thing was, the pram ...

was barking.

Chapter Two
Fried Egg and Pineapple

The next morning

everybody got up.

Gus and Gloria got up

and went to school.

Mr Gaskitt got up

and went shopping.

Mrs Gaskitt got up, got the paper,

got the post,

got a cup of tea

and a *cream doughnut* ...

and went back to bed.

Goodness me!

Meanwhile, Horace was out on the wall again

hoping to see and hear that

mysterious pram.

Well, Horace never saw

the pram that time,

but Mr Gaskitt did.

He was in his car at the school crossing

and there it was, the same as before,

with the same man just *whizzing* along.

But not barking, though. Oh, no!

It was more like ... squeaking,

Mr Gaskitt thought.

When Gus and Gloria got to school

they found that something

dreadful had happened.

Randolph – clever, lovable Randolph –

the class rat, had ("Squeak, squeak!") …

disappeared.

Oh yes, and Mrs Fritter,
while trying to find him,
had fallen out of a window.

The children, of course,

were terribly upset.

"Poor Randolph!" they cried.

"Poor Randolph!"

"Poor Randolph!"

Oh yes,
and poor
Mrs Fritter.

By this time Mr Gaskitt

was in the supermarket

filling his trolley.

Horace was visiting

a friend who *seemed*

to be out.

Mrs Gaskitt

was also out ...

of bed.

Hooray!

She was downstairs now in the sitting-room

watching TV, with a mug of hot chocolate

and a fried egg and pineapple –

Pineapple?

– yes, pineapple

sandwich.

Meanwhile, somewhere

not very far away,

that pram was …

… still whizzing along.

So, let's follow the pram, shall we? Here's a useful map. It shows where the pram has been so far this morning and where it's going.

Hm … and here's a big white van with a ramp. Now the pram is being pushed into the van.

Ha-ha!

What's going on here?

And look!
There's Horace on a
wall again, outside his
friend's house.

Horace is a smart cat.
Well, *Horace* thinks
he is. He's thinking
now that if he sits here
for a while, his friend
will show up ... or
something *interesting*
might happen.

It probably will.

Chapter Three
Meet Mr Cruncher

Back at school Gus and Gloria

and the other children

were in the classroom

whispering about Randolph –

"Poor Randolph!"

"Poor Randolph!"

– and waiting for the

supply teacher. (Mrs Fritter

– nasty cuts and bruises –

had gone home in a taxi.)

Suddenly – Bang! –

the classroom

door flew open,

the windows rattled,

the floor shook …

and there he was.

Very tall.

Very wide.

With a great big

heavy bag.

And his name was,

MR CRUNCHER!

Mr Cruncher was
a PE teacher,
a keep-fit fiend.
He had been in the army.
He had been in the navy.
He was a man of few
words … and he *loved*
running.

Mr Blagg, the headmaster,
shook hands with
Mr Cruncher –
Ooer!

– and wished he hadn't.

Mr Cruncher said, "Good morning, class!"

and the windows rattled again.

After that the lessons began.

During the morning

Mr Cruncher taught

reading, writing

and *running*.

But mostly running.

There were obstacle races

in the classroom, relay races

in the hall and laps and laps

And laps!

… on the school field.

Poor us!

By lunchtime
Gus and Gloria
and the others
had forgotten
Randolph,
and were puffing
and gasping
and sleeping even
… on the grass.

Poor us!

Poor us!

Meanwhile,

where's Horace?

He was on that wall

when we last saw him,

wasn't he?

But he's not there now.

Meanwhile also,

where's the pram?

Well, it's still

whizzing along – look!

Down the road,

round the corner,

up the ramp …

and into the van.

It seems a bit odd,

that pram, doesn't it?

Let's take a closer look.

29

Let's see what

sort of *baby*

it's got in there.

Let's see, closer,

closer,

and closer...

Oh, no –

Miaow!

– they've got

Horace!

Chapter Four
Have You Seen This Hamster?

By two o'clock that afternoon

trouble was brewing all over town.

There were cats missing,

and dogs missing,

gerbils,

guinea pigs – even goldfish!

Even budgerigars!

Even – well,

not just at this moment,

but fairly soon now – even *penguins!*

Yes, sad owners wandered

up and down the streets

whistling and calling,

"Here, Tibby!"

"Here, Marmaduke!"

"Here, Sweetie Pie!"

Some of them
put posters up,
HAVE YOU SEEN
THIS HAMSTER?
Some phoned
for the police.

Back at the school
the children heard
none of this.
All they knew about
was Randolph.

"Poor Randolph!"

HAVE YOU
SEEN THIS
HAMSTER?

call 01432 6578
with information

All they cared about was their sore feet.

For the literacy hour Mr Cruncher had them lifting heavy books.

In science he had them lifting ... each other!

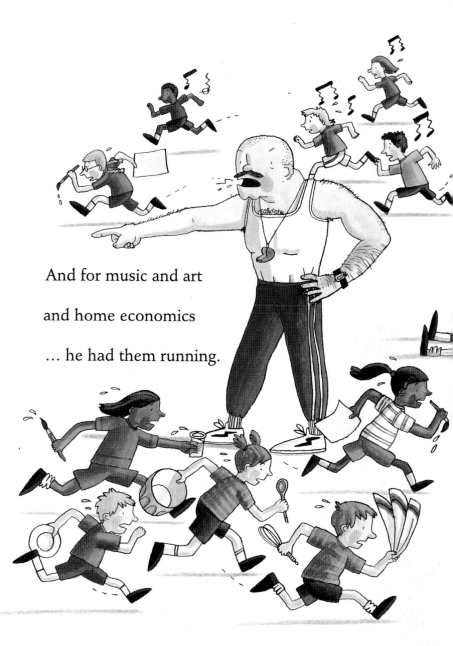

And for music and art

and home economics

… he had them running.

When they got home,
Gus and Gloria sat on
their mother's bed
and told her
all about it.

"It's dreadful,
Mum!"
"Our legs are
dropping off!"
"We're worn out!"

"Dear me," said Mrs Gaskitt,

or rather, "Drr ... mrr..."

She was eating a sandwich

at the time.

Yes, fried egg and

pineapple again.

Also, as you can see,

she was *in* bed again.

And it isn't even teatime.

Why is that?

Meanwhile, downstairs, Mr Gaskitt

was cooking the children's tea,

doing a bit of ironing and

listening to the radio.

"THE MYSTERY OF THE

MISSING PETS!"

yelled the radio.

"CATS AND DOGS

VANISHING INTO

THIN AIR!"

"POLICE

BAFFLED!"

Mr Gaskitt folded a shirt and put it on a pile. He looked in the oven, peered out of the window and opened the kitchen door.

"Hm." Mr Gaskitt gazed thoughtfully into the garden and rubbed his chin.

"Where's Horace?"

So where *is* Horace? Time, perhaps, for another useful map. This one shows where the van went with Horace in it. Ha-ha! Looks like they've taken him to the next town! It also shows (it's a *very* useful map) where the Number 9 bus goes.

MAP 2

N

CINEMA

BUS

SOSSO

NEXT TOWN

BUS

PET SHOP

KEY:
- - - - VAN ROUTE
> > > > > > BUS ROUTE
• • • • RUNNING ROUTE

HOSPITAL

BUS 6

That could come in handy. And where, tomorrow morning bright and early – actually, it's going to rain – Gus and Gloria and the others may very well, if Mr Cruncher gets his way, may very well … be *running*.

Chapter Five
Honest Joe

That night Gus and Gloria did not sleep a wink.

All they could think about was,

Poor Horace!

They had walked the streets

and knocked on doors

and looked *everywhere* …

but couldn't find him.

Mr and Mrs Gaskitt

– look, she's out of bed! –

had driven all round the town

and *they* couldn't find him.

Meanwhile, in the *next* town ...

in the back room of a pet shop

a large number of unhappy pets

were barking

and squealing

and twittering

and so on,

hoping to be let out.

Upstairs above the shop Honest Joe was

playing cards with his

honest mother and his

honest Uncle Sid.

Pet shop? *Pet* shop?

What's going on here?

And who's "Honest Joe"?

Well, Honest Joe –

it's time now you were told –

thinks of himself as a sort of *pet collector*.

He rescues animals, or so he says,

that are lost or strayed

and finds them nice

new cosy homes.

His mother and his uncle

help him in this work.

Usually they travel

round from town to town,

open a little shop for a while,

make a little money,

play a little cards …

and travel on.

Honest Joe means no harm.

He would not hurt a fly

– or so he says –

or a gerbil …

or a cat.

The worst he'd ever do

is put them in a shop –

Oh no, poor Horace! –

and sell them.

Chapter Six
The Great Escape

It was half past six in the morning.

Horace Gaskitt sat in the window

of Honest Joe's Pet Shop,

watching the world go by.

Horace was a brainy cat.

Well, Horace thought he was.

He was thinking now,

and had been thinking

since Honest Uncle Sid had grabbed him,

he was thinking now ... how to escape.

Meanwhile, in the window next to

Horace – sat Randolph!

He was thinking of escaping too.

"What we need is a plan," said Horace.

"We could dig a tunnel, maybe –

or get a glass-cutter!"

"Hm." Randolph said nothing,

but rubbed his little chin.

Randolph, you see, really *was* brainy.

He lived in a school after all.

Randolph was educated.

RAt
£ 2

Horace now was getting carried away.

"It could be great!" he cried. "Like that movie –

The Great Escape!

We could be famous –

on TV – wow!"

And he said (or rather yelled),

"We could make a rope ladder!

We could disguise ourselves!"

"No," said Randolph.

He was studying the

wire pen they were in.

"I've got a better idea.

Wake that guinea pig up."

The guinea pig's name was Maurice,

and he was not really asleep,

just fed up.

"It's hopeless," he groaned.

"We'll never get out."

"Yes, we will," said Randolph.

"Climb on Horace's back."

"What for?" said Maurice,

but he did it anyway.

And then – look at that!

Randolph, clever Randolph,

climbs up on Maurice's back

(on his head, actually),

RAt
£2

and

stretches

and

stretches

and

stretches up …

to the catch …

on the door …

of the pen.

Chapter Seven
That Pram Again

Now the pace is quickening.

Now things are hotting up.

Now ... well, you get the idea.

Anyway, here's the TIMETABLE

6:45

Horace, Maurice and Randolph tiptoe – Sh! – out of the shop window.

7:30

Honest Joe, Mrs Gaskitt, Mrs Fritter and Mr Cruncher have their breakfasts. In different places, of course.

8:15

Honest Joe's mother loads the pram into the van and drives off with Honest Uncle Sid.

At the same time, Horace, Maurice and Randolph creep out through the open door and run off down the street.

8:55

Gus and Gloria and the others get changed for their cross-country run.

The rain begins to fall. Five minutes later, Mrs Fritter falls too,

Poor Mrs Fritter!

tripping up over a rug on her way to the bathroom.

9:15

Uncle Sid takes his "baby" for a stroll in the *zoo*.

The Number 9 bus, meanwhile, leaves Fish Street – eight minutes late.

9:30

Mrs Gaskitt sits up in bed. She has a funny look on her face. Can you see? She looks happy and sad at the same time.

Why is that?

9:45

Mr Cruncher and his class are off – "Puff, gasp!" – on their run.

At the same time, down a little street at the back of the zoo – look, here it comes! – that pram again, with Honest Uncle Sid

… just *whizzing* along.

Chapter Eight
Clever Randolph!

Horace, Maurice and Randolph

were hiding behind a litter bin

next to a bus shelter.

Randolph was thoughtful.

Maurice was gloomy.

And Horace …

was getting carried away.

"It's like in that movie!" he cried.

"*The Incredible Journey* – where these pets

travel thousands and thousands of miles

to get back home!"

"Was one of them a guinea pig?" said Maurice.

"Can't remember," said Horace.

"Anyway, we could do that!
Hide out in a barn –
follow the stars
at night ... have
adventures."

But Randolph
only coughed
and rubbed his
little chin.
"No," he said.
"I've got a
better idea."

Meanwhile, outside the zoo,

Honest Uncle Sid was whizzing along

with a pramful of penguins.

Yes – penguins!

He was supposed to get *parrots*

but Uncle Sid had always

wanted a penguin.

Or two.

Or eight.

Anyway, there he was,

whizzing along,

when who should

he spy outside the scout hut

but a little tiny tied-up spotted dozy ... dog.

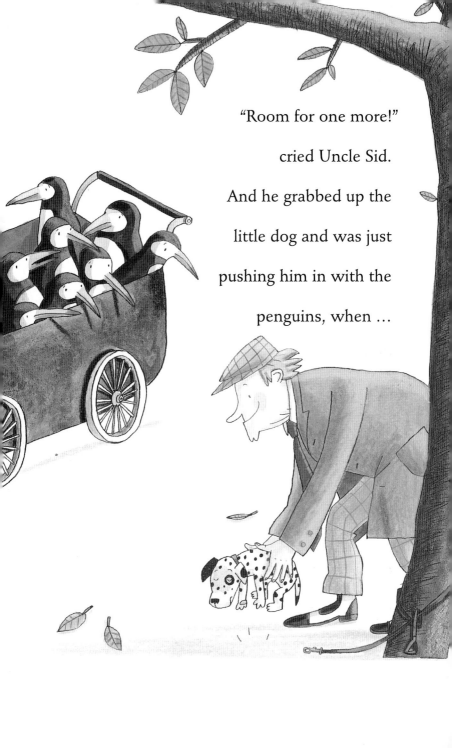

"Room for one more!"

cried Uncle Sid.

And he grabbed up the

little dog and was just

pushing him in with the

penguins, when …

round the corner came

Gus and Gloria and

Tracey and Billy and a few others.

Meanwhile also,

Goodness me!

Mr and Mrs Gaskitt were driving by.

They spotted Gus and Gloria and waved …

but couldn't stop. Mr Gaskitt was

taking Mrs Gaskitt – Oh, no! –

to the hospital.

What's wrong?

Is she poorly?

She doesn't look poorly.

Meanwhile *also*, the

Number 9 bus was…

But things are getting

a bit complicated,

don't you think?

Perhaps we

could do with …

one more map.

See – there's the pram with the van parked round the corner.

There's Gus and Gloria and the others, including Mr Cruncher.

There's Mr and Mrs Gaskitt in their car.

There's the Number 9 bus.

And there –
can you see? –
upstairs on the
bus, on the front
seat, side by side,
cosy, safe and
sharing a bag of
crisps they've
found ...

there's Horace,
and Maurice
and ...
clever
Randolph.

Chapter Nine
Running Like the Wind

But what happened
next, you'll say.
Hm … well,
let's see.

Uncle Sid
whizzed off
with his once
more barking
pram. (That

little dozy
dog was wide
awake now.)

Like a rocket he
went, round

the corner,

down
the street,
up the ramp,
into the van …
and away.

64

And after him

came Gus

and Gloria

and Billy

and Tracey.

And Marigold

and Mary

and Tom

and Rupert

and Buster

and Polly

and Esmeralda

and Mr Cruncher ...

and a few others.

So the race

began. The race?

Race? Between

a van and children?

Yes – and it was much

closer than you'd think.

See – the children

were young, strong,

and ran like the wind.

Mr Cruncher was

proud of them.

65

Meanwhile, the van was old, stolen and
had failed its MOT.

So what with traffic-lights and
zebra crossings and so on, Gus and Gloria
and the others

kept up with it …

down this road,

down that,

up this hill,

over that bridge …

all the way to

the next town.

All the way, in fact, to *Honest Joe's.*

Honest Joe, meanwhile,

was hard at work serving

a customer.

Suddenly in burst

his honest mother,

his honest uncle,

a grumpy little

barking dog,

four or five penguins –

"Penguins!" cried Joe.

"Where's the parrots?" –

and a whole

classful of hot

and steaming …

"KIDS!"

Not to mention

Mr Cruncher.

Then the *battle* began.

Well, it wasn't

much of a battle.

Honest Joe's mother

tried to sneak off,

but tripped up over a

penguin and was sat on

by some of the bigger girls.

And the penguin.

Honest Joe punched Mr Cruncher in the tummy –

Ooer!

– and wished he hadn't.

Honest Uncle Sid looked at the odds, shrugged his shoulders and surrendered.

Meanwhile, at the hospital, Mrs Gaskitt was

in bed *again*. A doctor with a stethoscope

was listening to *her* tummy. Hm. What's going

on here? Let's have a listen too.

Shall we?

Sh…

"Where am I?

What's happening?

It's very dark in here.

I could just eat a doughnut.

Oh – here we go!

It's getting lighter...

Where? Where...

Waaaa!"

So there we are. (Did you guess?)

At half past one in the afternoon

on a Wednesday

in September

Mrs Gaskitt (and Mr Gaskitt too)

had – their – baby.

Little Gary Gaskitt:
brown hair
blue eyes
7lb 12oz

Congratulations!

Chapter Ten
The Final Timetable

Now the pace is slowing.

Now things are winding down.

Now ... well, you get the idea.

Anyway, here's the final

TIMETABLE

1:30

Little Gary Gaskitt arrives.

1:45

The police arrive (not at the hospital, though) and load Honest Joe and his gang into a van.

The police are happy. They have captured some dangerous criminals – and got their dog back.

Hello, Sweetie Pie

2:15

Meanwhile, Gus and Gloria and the other children are sad.
All these rescued pets, but where's Horace? Where's Randolph? And where (if they'd only ever heard of him), where's Maurice?

2:40

The children arrive ... back at the school.

Hooray!

Hooray!

Hooray!

There they are!

4:00

In the police cell Honest Joe and his mother play a little cards ...

and win a little money.

5:30

Mrs Fritter watches TV and thinks of going back to school.

Mr Cruncher goes off for an early evening run with his girlfriend.

At the same time, Mr Gaskitt drives Gus and Gloria and Horace to the hospital ... for the happy ending.

And the happy beginning!

Chapter Eleven
Meanwhile...

One week later the Gaskitts –

all five of them –

were at home sitting

side by side on the sofa.

All except little Gary.

He was in his carrycot.

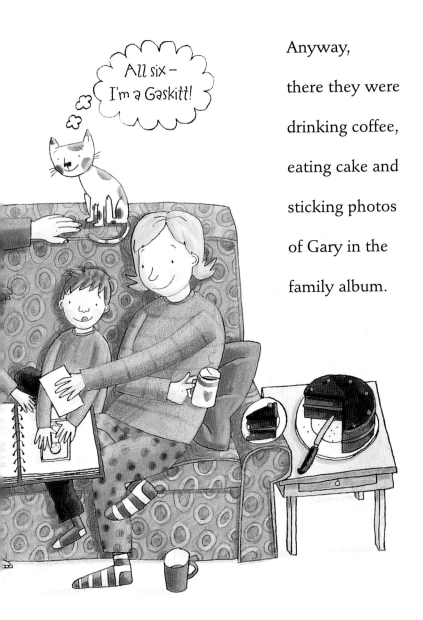

Anyway,

there they were

drinking coffee,

eating cake and

sticking photos

of Gary in the

family album.

There was a photo of Gary –

aged one hour,

a photo of Gary –

aged one day,

a photo of Gary –

aged two days ...

and so on.

Meanwhile, little Gary himself just lies there

in his cot and watches the world go by.

Gary Gaskitt is a clever baby.

(Well, Mrs Gaskitt thinks he is.)

He's thinking now

that if he lies there

long enough, something –

Yawn!

– something

interesting

might happen.

It probably will.

Bye-bye!